LADYBIRD BOOKS, INC.
Auburn, Maine 04210 U.S.A.
© LADYBIRD BOOKS LTD MCMLXXXVII
Loughborough, Leicestershire, England

Printed in U.S.A.

The Little Red Hen

Adapted by DONNA R. PARNELL
Illustrated by DEBORAH COLVIN BORGO

Ladybird Books

Once there was a little red hen.

One day, she found some grains of wheat.

The little red hen asked her friends,
"Who will help me plant this wheat?"

"Not I," said the cat.
"Not I," said the dog.
"Not I," said the pig.

"Then I will plant the wheat myself," said the little red hen.

And she did.

The little red hen
watched the wheat grow.
Soon it was tall and golden.

She asked her friends,
"Who will help me cut this wheat?"

"Not I," said the cat.
"Not I," said the dog.
"Not I," said the pig.

"Then I will cut the wheat myself,"
said the little red hen.
And she did.

It was time to make the wheat
into flour.
"Who will help me take
this wheat to the miller?"
asked the little red hen.

"Not I," said the cat.
"Not I," said the dog.
"Not I," said the pig.

"Then I will take it
to the miller myself,"
said the little red hen.

And she did.

The miller ground the wheat.

He put the flour in a sack
for the little red hen.

Now it was time to make
the flour into bread.
"Who will help me bake the bread?"
asked the little red hen.

"Not I," said the cat.
"Not I," said the dog.
"Not I," said the pig.

"Then I will bake the bread myself," said the little red hen.

And she did.

When the bread was baked,
the little red hen
took it out of the oven.
It looked delicious.
"Who will help me eat this bread?"
she asked.

"I will!" said the cat.
"I will!" said the dog.
"I will!" said the pig.

"No, you will not,"
said the little red hen.
"I will eat this bread myself."

And she did.